BOOGIE in the BRONX!

words by **Jackie Azúa kramer**

art by **Jana Glatt**

music by **Brian Amador** sung by **Sol y Canto**

Barefoot Books
Step inside a story

On sunny days to cool the heat,
Something happens to my feet.
Step left and right — I feel the groove.
Snap and tap! I've got the moves.

Music pumpin' from 4B,
People jumpin' in 6D.

Step left and right — they feel it too.
Snap and tap is what they do.

One barista wakes from his siesta,
Turns up the radio and starts the fiesta.
Snapping fingers, tapping toes!
Shake-shake-shake is how it goes.

Let's dance!
¡Vamos a bailar!*
*VAH-mos ah by-LAR

1
Uno*
*OOH-noh

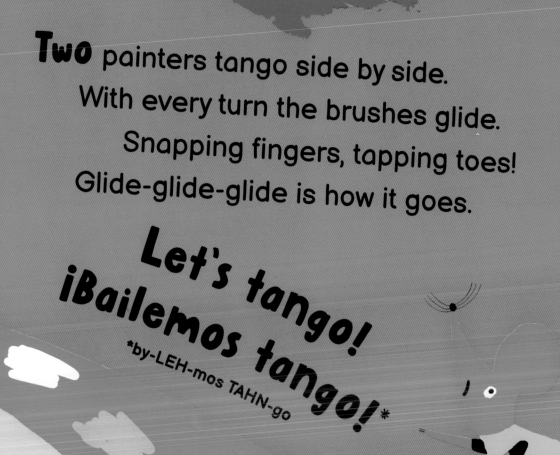

Two painters tango side by side.
With every turn the brushes glide.
Snapping fingers, tapping toes!
Glide-glide-glide is how it goes.

Let's tango!
¡Bailemos tango!*

*by-LEH-mos TAHN-go

2
Dos*

*dohs

Three chefs salsa as they grill.
Shimmying, slicing — that takes skill!
Snapping fingers, tapping toes!
Shimmy-shimmy-shimmy is how it goes.

Let's salsa!
¡Bailemos salsa!*
*by-LEH-mos SAHL-sah

3
Tres*
*trehs

Four firefighters join the fun,
And roll their hips to reggaeton.
Snapping fingers, tapping toes!
Roll-roll-roll is how it goes.

Let's body wave!
¡Bailemos el body wave!*
*by-LEH-mos ell BO-dee weyf

4
Cuatro*
*KWAT-roh

Five nurses samba fast.
Bodies tilting, they have a blast.
Snapping fingers, tapping toes!
Fast-fast-fast is how it goes.

Let's samba!
¡Bailemos samba!*
*by-LEH-mos SAHM-bah

5
Cinco*
*SEEN-koh

Six musicians love to swing.
To cumbia's drum they do their thing.
Snapping fingers, tapping toes!
Swing-swing-swing is how it goes.

Let's cumbia!
¡Bailemos cumbia!*

*by-LEH-mos KOOM-bya

**6
Seis***

*seyss

Seven athletes put on a show.
To mambo's beat they turn and flow.
Snapping fingers, tapping toes!
Turn-turn-turn is how it goes.

Let's mambo!
¡Bailemos mambo!*
*by-LEH-mos MAHM-boh

7
Siete*
*SYEH-teh

Eight breakers bounce and bop,
To rhymin' beats in cool hip-hop.
Snapping fingers, tapping toes!
Bounce-bounce-bounce is how it goes.

Let's two-step!
¡Bailemos el *two-step!**

*by-LEH-mos ell too-STEP

**8
Ocho***

*OH-choh

Nine sopranos rumba slow,
Feathers swayin' to and fro.
Snapping fingers, tapping toes!
Sway-sway-sway is how it goes.

Let's rumba!
¡Bailemos rumba!*
*by-LEH-mos ROOM-bah

9
Nueve*
*NWEH-veh

Ten children whirl and wiggle.
Merengue makes them smile and giggle.
Snapping fingers, tapping toes!
Wiggle-wiggle-wiggle is how it goes.

Let's merengue!
¡Bailemos merengue!*

*by-LEH-mos meh-RENG-geh

10
Diez*

*dyess

A conga line forms after me.
Count **one** to **ten** and you will see.
Snapping fingers, tapping toes!
Kick-kick-kick is how it goes.

Let's conga!
¡Bailemos conga!*

*by-LEH-mos KONG-gah

TACOS

BRONX ZOO

COLD DRINKS

BRONX   OPEN 24 HOURS   BRONX

Down to the street we make our way,
And dance until the end of day.
Snapping fingers, tapping toes!
Step left and right is how it goes.

**Let's dance!
¡Vamos a bailar!***

*VAH-mos ah by-LAR

About The Bronx

The Bronx is one of New York City's five boroughs. It's home to the New York Yankees baseball team, New York's Botanical Garden and the famous Bronx Zoo. There are over 75 different languages spoken by the people who live there, though English and Spanish are the most common. It's also where hip-hop music was first created!

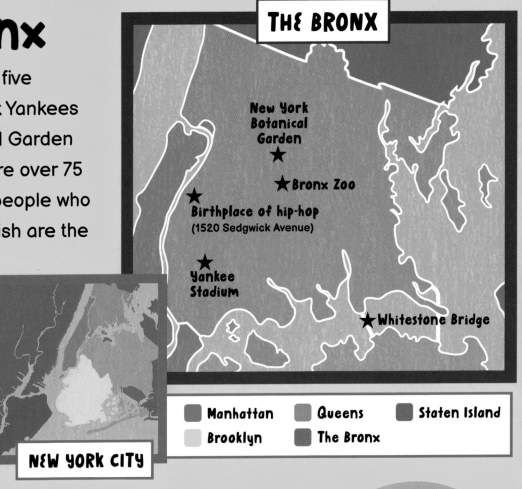

THE BRONX

New York Botanical Garden ★

★ Bronx Zoo

★ Birthplace of hip-hop
(1520 Sedgwick Avenue)

★ Yankee Stadium

★ Whitestone Bridge

	Manhattan		Queens		Staten Island
	Brooklyn		The Bronx		

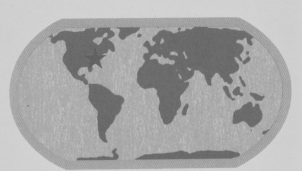

NEW YORK CITY

Author's Note

As a kid in New York City, I loved visiting the amazing Bronx Zoo, and later I took my own kids there. Directly across the street from the zoo are apartment buildings. During one summertime visit to the zoo, the sound of different types of music pouring out of those apartments gave me an idea. Having grown up in a Latinx family, some of my most vivid memories are of the parties my parents threw almost every weekend. It's where I learned to dance to the music of salsa, cumbia and merengue. So this book became a celebration of the diverse music, dance and sounds of the Boogie-Down Bronx. Can you find the illustration of the animals dancing in the Bronx Zoo? — **Jackie Azúa Kramer**

About the Dances

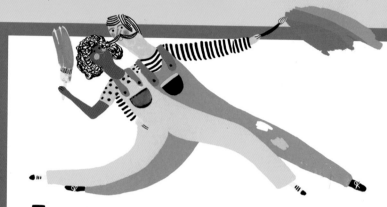

Tango is a playful partner dance that originated in Argentina and Uruguay. It has a lot of side-by-side movement.

Salsa combines different styles of Cuban and American dances. Dancers shimmy, shake and tap to music that's also called salsa.

Reggaeton is a rhythmic music genre that came from Panama and was made popular in Puerto Rico. Dancers roll their hips, bounce their shoulders up and down and do body waves to the beat.

Samba is a fast and lively dance of Afro-Brazilian origin with simple forward and backward steps and tilting, rocking body movements.

Cumbia is a simple dance with a forward and backward swinging motion. It is often danced in a circular pattern alone or with a partner.

Mambo is an exciting, energetic ballroom dance with strong hip movements, quick footwork and partner turns.

Hip-hop is a culture created in the Bronx defined by rapping, break dancing, graffiti and DJing / turntabling. Breakers often do the two-step while dancing to hip-hop music, in which they take two steps in the same direction on the same foot then step in the opposite direction with the other foot.

Rumba is a ballroom dance where couples sway slowly in place. In this book, it's being danced by a group of sopranos, who are singers with very high voices.

Merengue is the national dance of the Dominican Republic. Dancers wiggle their hips in a light and playful way.

Conga dancers form a long line that eventually becomes a circle. They take three steps on the beat, followed by a kick.

Illustrator's Note

The illustrations for this book were inspired by my childhood in Brazil. Like the Bronx, Rio de Janeiro is a place filled with different kinds of music and dance — especially samba! I love to illustrate bright, busy scenes of happy people, so this book is a perfect fit for my style. To create my artwork, I start with liquid water-based paints, pencils and crayons. Then I use a computer to put the pieces together. When I look at the finished artwork, I am especially proud of the diversity I see in the people — another thing Rio and the Bronx have in common! — **Jana Glatt**

BOOGIE in the BRONX!

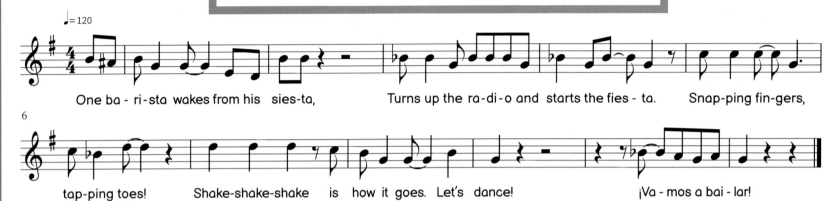

♩=120

One ba - ri-sta wakes from his sies-ta, Turns up the ra-di-o and starts the fies - ta. Snap-ping fin-gers,

tap-ping toes! Shake-shake-shake is how it goes. Let's dance! ¡Va - mos a bai - lar!

To Preston and all the littles everywhere who are born loving to boogie! — **J.A.K.**

To my daughter Malú, who loves dance, music and books.
I hope you enjoy this one! — **J.G.**

Barefoot Books would like to thank María-Verónica A. Barnes, Director of Diversity Education at Lexington Montessori School; Anne Cohen, disability consultant; Dr. Melody Ann Ross, pronunciation consultant; and Lilia Weisfeldt, dance consultant, for their expert input in the creation of this book.

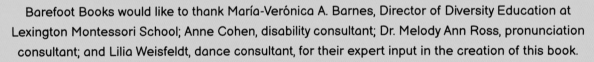

Barefoot Books
23 Bradford Street, 2nd Floor
Concord, MA 01742

Barefoot Books
29/30 Fitzroy Square
London, W1T 6LQ

Text copyright © 2023 by Jackie Azúa Kramer
Illustrations copyright © 2023 by Jana Glatt
The moral rights of Jackie Azúa Kramer and Jana Glatt have been asserted

Performed by Sol y Canto featuring Brian Amador, guitar, vocals;
Rosi Amador, vocals; Daniel Cantor, drums; Gonzalo Grau, keyboards, programming;
Akili Jamal Haynes, trumpet; Paul Lieberman, alto sax, flute; Mikael Ringquist, percussion
Musical arrangement ℗ 2023 by Brian Amador, Greñudo Music (BMI)
Produced by Sol y Canto, Boston, USA
Recorded, mixed and mastered by Daniel Cantor at Notable Productions
Animation by Collaborate Agency, UK
First published in the United States of America by Barefoot Books, Inc
and in Great Britain by Barefoot Books, Ltd in 2023. All rights reserved

Graphic design by Elizabeth Jayasekera and Sarah Soldano, Barefoot Books
Edited and art directed by Emma Parkin and Bree Reyes, Barefoot Books
Reproduction by Bright Arts, Hong Kong. Printed in China
This book was typeset in Balsamiq Sans and Stomping Grounds
The illustrations were prepared in liquid water-based paint, pencils and crayon

Hardback ISBN 979-8-88859-000-3 | Paperback ISBN 979-8-88859-001-0
E-book ISBN 979-8-88859-037-9

British Cataloguing-in-Publication Data: a catalogue record for this book
is available from the British Library

Library of Congress Cataloging-in-Publication Data
is available under LCCN 2023935232

1 3 5 7 9 8 6 4 2

Go to **www.barefootbooks.com/boogiebronx** to access your audio singalong and video animation online.

Barefoot Books
Step inside a story

At Barefoot Books, we celebrate art and story that opens the hearts
and minds of children from all walks of life, focusing on themes that
encourage independence of spirit, enthusiasm for learning and respect
for the world's diversity. The welfare of our children is dependent on
the welfare of the planet, so we source paper from sustainably managed
forests and constantly strive to reduce our environmental impact.
Playful, beautiful and created to last a lifetime, our products combine
the best of the present with the best of the past to educate our
children as the caretakers of tomorrow.

www.barefootbooks.com

Jackie Azúa Kramer was born in New York City. She is the author of many books for children, and her writing has been translated into more than a dozen languages. Jackie has also worked as an actor, singer and school counselor. Her work with children inspired her to address their concerns, secrets and hopes through storytelling. Today, Jackie lives with her family in Long Island, New York, USA. www.jackieazuakramer.com.

Jana Glatt's fascination with creating characters, costumes and scenarios began in her childhood theatre classes. Today, she feels like a director of a great scene when she is creating her illustrations. Jana has illustrated more than twenty books, and her art has been seen all over the world. She lives in Rio de Janeiro, Brazil.

Sol y Canto is the award-winning Pan-Latin ensemble led by Puerto Rican/Argentine singer and percussionist Rosi Amador and New Mexican guitarist and composer **Brian Amador**. Featuring Rosi's crystalline voice and Brian's lush Spanish guitar and inventive compositions, Sol y Canto is known for making their music accessible to Spanish- and English-speaking audiences of all ages. They live in Cambridge, Massachusetts, USA.